IMMORTALS VS. NAVY SEALS

Disclaimer:
The battles in this book are not real. It is fun to imagine. These 2 opponents would never fight each other in real life.

45th Parallel Press

Published in the United States of America by Cherry Lake Publishing
Ann Arbor, Michigan
www.cherrylakepublishing.com

Reading Adviser: Marla Conn, MS, Ed., Literacy specialist, Read-Ability, Inc.
Book Designer: Melinda Millward

Photo Credits: © Getmilitaryphotos/Shutterstock.com, back cover, cover, 5, 16; © Iunstream / Alamy Stock Photo, cover, 5; © Borna_Mirahmadian/Shutterstock.com, 6; © North Wind Picture Archives, 9; © Sammy33/Shutterstock.com, 10; © U.S. Navy, 12, 15, 19, 27; © GraphicsRF/Shutterstock.com, 19, 20; © vectortatu/Shutterstock.com, 20; © Heritage Image/ age fotostock, 21; © Oleg Zabielin/Dreamstime.com, 23; © denniro/Shutterstock.com, 24; © Firouzime/Dreamstime.com, 25; © NNehring/istock, 25; © CC7/Shutterstock.com, 29

Graphic Element Credits: © studiostoks/Shutterstock.com, back cover, multiple interior pages; © infostocker/Shutterstock.com, back cover, multiple interior pages; © mxbfilms/Shutterstock.com, front cover; © MF production/Shutterstock.com, front cover, multiple interior pages; © AldanNi/Shutterstock.com, front cover, multiple interior pages; © Andrii Symonenko/Shutterstock.com, front cover, multiple interior pages; © acidmit/Shutterstock.com, front cover, multiple interior pages; © manop/Shutterstock.com, multiple interior pages; © Lina Kalina/Shutterstock.com, multiple interior pages; © mejorana/Shutterstock.com, multiple interior pages; © NoraVector/Shutterstock.com, multiple interior pages; © Smirnov Viacheslav/Shutterstock.com, multiple interior pages; © Piotr Urakau/Shutterstock.com, multiple interior pages; © IMOGI graphics/Shutterstock.com, multiple interior pages; © jirawat phueksriphan/Shutterstock.com, multiple interior pages

Copyright © 2020 by Cherry Lake Publishing

All rights reserved. No part of this book may be reproduced or utilized in any form or by any means without written permission from the publisher.

45th Parallel Press is an imprint of Cherry Lake Publishing.

Library of Congress Cataloging-in-Publication Data

Names: Loh-Hagan, Virginia, author.
Title: Immortals vs. Navy SEALs / by Virginia Loh-Hagan.
Description: [Ann Arbor : Cherry Lake Publishing, 2019] | Series: Battle royale : lethal warriors | Includes bibliographical references and index. | Audience: Grades: 4-6.
Identifiers: LCCN 2019003641| ISBN 9781534147676 (hardcover) | ISBN 9781534150539 (pbk.) | ISBN 9781534149106 (pdf) | ISBN 9781534151963 (hosted ebook)
Subjects: LCSH: Imaginary wars and battles—Juvenile literature. | Soldiers—Juvenile literature. | United States. Navy. SEALs—Juvenile literature. | Iran—History, Military—Juvenile literature. | Achaemenid dynasty, 559-330 B.C.—Juvenile literature.
Classification: LCC U313 .L64 2019 | DDC 355.00935/709014—dc23
LC record available at https://lccn.loc.gov/2019003641

Printed in the United States of America
Corporate Graphics

About the Author

Dr. Virginia Loh-Hagan is an author, university professor, former classroom teacher, and curriculum designer. She lives close to the Navy SEALs training base. She has friends who are Navy SEALs. She lives in San Diego with her very tall husband and very naughty dogs. To learn more about her, visit www.virginialoh.com.

Table of Contents

Introduction 4
Immortals 6
Navy SEALs 12
Choose Your Battleground 18
Fight On! 22
And the Victor Is... 28

Consider This! 32
Learn More! 32
Glossary 32
Index 32

Introduction

Imagine a battle between Immortals and Navy SEALs. Who would win? Who would lose?

Enter the world of *Battle Royale: Lethal* **Warriors**! Warriors are fighters. This is a fight to the death! The last team standing is the **victor**! Victors are winners. They get to live.

Opponents are fighters who compete against each other. They challenge each other. They fight with everything they've got. They use weapons. They use their special skills. They use their powers.

They're not fighting for prizes. They're not fighting for honor. They're not fighting for their countries. They're fighting for their lives. Victory is their only option.

Let the games begin!

In real life, nobody really wins in a war.

IMMORTALS

Immortals were also called Persian Immortals or Persian Warriors.

Immortals were soldiers. **Immortal** means not being able to die. It means living forever. Immortals were **Persian**. Today, Persia is called Iran. It's in the Middle East. Immortals helped conquer lands. They helped build the largest empire in the area. The Persian Empire was huge. Its first ruler was Cyrus the Great. Cyrus created the Immortals.

Immortals were an **imperial** guard. Imperial means of the empire. Immortals protected the king. They were the king's bodyguards. They were an **elite** fighting group. Elite means a select group that is superior to others. Immortals were the ancient world's special forces. They were killing machines. They were trained to kill and destroy.

From birth, boys were hidden away. They couldn't see their fathers. They grew until age 5. Then, they started training. They learned **archery**. Archery is the ability to shoot bows and arrows. Persian boys learned fighting skills. They learned to live off the land. They learned to march long distances. They learned to tame and ride animals. They served in the military from ages 15 to 50.

There were exactly 10,000 soldiers in the Immortals. Men retired. They were killed. They were hurt. As this happened, these men were removed. They were taken off battlefields. They were replaced by a new Immortal. This made it look like the men couldn't be killed.

Immortal officers had gold fruit on top of their spears.

Immortals wore leather over their chests. They wore caps to keep out wind and dust. They had **wicker** shields covered in leather. Wicker is woven wood strips. Immortals had spears. They had swords. They had small knives. They had bows and arrows. They traveled with covered wagons. Their wagons carried their things. They carried their servants. Immortals rode on horses, camels, and elephants.

Immortals fought together. They worked as one. They were strong. They were smart. They were well-equipped. They were part of a bigger Persian army. They were called in at special moments. Persian forces were well-formed. They were highly trained. They struck fear in their enemies' hearts.

FUN FACTS ABOUT IMMORTALS

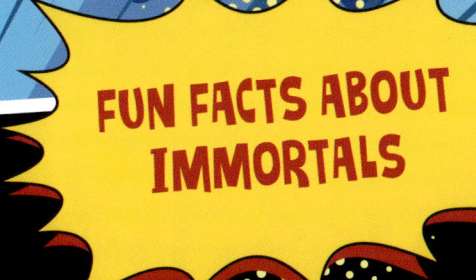

- Immortals were part of a huge army. It was hard to move everyone. So, Immortals had a lot of time to hang out. They hunted in their free time. They hunted big cats. Big cats include lions, panthers, and cheetahs. Immortals hunted to practice fighting. They wore animal skins.

- Cyrus the Great may have created the first human rights charter. Charters are pacts. Cyrus's army took over Babylon. He created the Cyrus Cylinder. This was an object made of baked clay. The words on it talked about equality for all.

- There's a movie called 300. It was made in 2006. It's about a battle between Spartans and Persians. Spartans are ancient Greeks. The movie is about the Battle of Thermopylae. Persians invaded Greece. Spartans blocked Persians. They lost. But they held them off for several days.

- Immortals modeled themselves after Sparabara. Sparabara were Persian foot soldiers. They were the first to fight in battles. They fought with spears and shields. They formed shield walls. They used their spears to protect archers.

NAVY SEALS

Navy SEALs were established by President John F. Kennedy in 1962.

Navy SEALs are an elite fighting force. They perform special operations. They work for the U.S. Navy. They protect citizens. SEAL stands for sea, air, land. They're trained fighters. They can fight in the sea, air, and land. They're men of honor. Their minds and bodies are strong. They're fit. They're smart.

They work in small teams. Teams have 1 to 16 people. Navy SEALs do specific jobs. They often work in top secret. They plan. They prepare. They can work anywhere. They can do anything. They train in deserts. They train in jungles. They train in cities. They train in cold and hot weather. Nothing scares them.

Navy SEALs gather information. They spy. They plant bugs. They find their enemies. They study their enemies. They study target areas. They do a lot of research.

They use **guerilla warfare**. They don't fight in battlefields. They fight as small groups. They're always on the move. They destroy enemy supplies. They distract. They do sneak attacks. They blow things up. They hit and run. But they never leave one of their own behind.

They rescue. They do direct attacks. They target enemies. They take out enemies. They also work with their enemies' enemies. They organize secret meetings. They train others how to fight.

Support groups help Navy SEALs.

Navy SEALs are either working or training. SEAL training is the world's toughest military training. Only 25 percent of people complete it. Not everyone can be a SEAL.

SEALs learn fighting skills. They swim in cold water. They swim with their hands and feet tied. They dive. They carry heavy loads. They run. They learn survival skills. They learn to operate without sleep. They work with bombs and weapons. They work with boats. They learn to jump out of planes. They learn to drive fast. They learn to spy. They learn about teamwork. They learn to not be afraid. They learn to be tough.

FUN FACTS ABOUT NAVY SEALS

- There's a Navy SEAL museum. It's in Fort Pierce, Florida. It's on the original training grounds of the Navy combat divers. It was founded in 1985. A goal is to preserve the Navy SEALs' history. Another goal is to honor Navy SEALs who died.

- Navy SEALs say, "The only easy day was yesterday." This is their motto. A motto is a saying. It represents a group's beliefs.

- Navy SEALs also train dogs. These dogs are called war dogs. They help in secret missions. Navy SEALs' dog of choice is the Belgian Malinois. These dogs hide and find bombs. They sniff out safe areas. They're fast runners.

- Navy SEALs have several nicknames. They fought in the Vietnam War. The Vietnamese called them "the men with green faces." This is because Navy SEALs wore green paint. Navy SEALs did this to blend in.

- Women are now allowed to apply to be Navy SEALs. This happened in 2016. Since then, a few women have tried out. Their names are protected.

CHOOSE YOUR BATTLEGROUND

Immortals and Navy SEALs are fierce fighters. They're well-matched. They're the best of the best. They're both elite fighting forces. They both have a lot of war training. They both have special skills. But they have different ways of fighting. So, choose your battleground carefully!

Battleground #1: Sea

- Immortals mainly fight on land. They travel to different lands. Their ships carry their things. They can't swim. They hire Persian sailors to work the seas.

- Navy SEALs are best at sea. They're good swimmers. They're good divers. They use boats. They're expert seamen. They have a lot of experience fighting at sea.

People can go to the city of Coronado in California. They can watch SEALs train on the beach.

Battleground #2: Land

- Immortals are great land fighters. That's their strength. Immortals can march for a long time. They're close to their supplies. They're close to their horses.

- Navy SEALs know how to fight on land. They use the land. They **camouflage**. Camouflage means to blend in. They hide. They attack.

Battleground #3: Mountains

- Immortals march across different lands. They won't be able to get their wagons up mountains.

- Navy SEALs train to fight on all land types. **Rugged** land doesn't scare them. Rugged is uneven and rocky. Navy SEALs can climb. They can also jump out of planes. They're used to being high and in the air.

ARMED AND DANGEROUS: WEAPONS

Immortals: Immortals used the sagaris. The sagaris has a long handle. It has a metal head. The head has two sides. One side is pointy and sharp. It's like an ice pick. The other side could be different. Some sagaris sides are like battle-axes. They have sharp blades. Some sagaris sides are like war hammers. They have blunt edges. Sagaris could slash through iron and bronze armor. It was light. It could be used with one hand. It was swung over the head.

Navy SEALs: Navy SEALs use hand grenades. Grenades are used at short range. They kill within 15 feet (4.6 meters). They maim at 45 feet (14 m). Maim means to damage the body. They can send hot metal bits as far as 250 feet (76 m). Navy SEALs hold grenades. They pull out a plug. They throw the grenades. They do this to clear rooms. They do this to blow up people and things. This lets Navy SEALs move around.

FIGHT ON!

The battle begins! Navy SEALs spied on the Persian king. They learned that Persians want to grow their empire. The Immortals have kidnapped the U.S. president. They make demands. They want U.S. land. They want California. The Navy SEALs fight back. They plan a rescue. They plan an attack.

Move 1:

A team of Navy SEALs is dropped from a plane. They **parachute** down. Parachutes are tools with umbrella tops. They're used to slow down a sky fall. Navy SEALs land in woods. They land close to the Persians' camp. Another group of Navy SEALs swim in from a ship. They're on the beach. They're on the other side of the Persians' camp. This all happens at midnight.

Navy SEALs are also called frogmen. Frogmen are people who trained in swimming underwater.

Move 2:

Persian soldiers are on watch. They see the plane. They see the ship. They don't see any SEALs. But they're **suspicious**. Suspicious means they're mistrustful. Persian soldiers run. They tell the Immortals. Immortals prepare for battle. They spread the news. They get dressed. They wear their weapons. They get ready to march.

Move 3:

The team that dropped from the plane goes to the Persians' camp. They stay low. They're wearing **night vision goggles**. These are special glasses. They let them see in the dark. The SEAL team looks for the president. They were told not to attack. They're on a learning mission. Their task is to rescue.

Navy SEAL training is called Basic Underwater Demolition/ SEAL (BUD/S).

LIFE SOURCE: FOOD FOR BATTLE

Immortals: Immortals served Darius I. Darius I was the fourth king of the Persian Empire. In the 6th century BCE, his soldiers went on long marches. They needed quick and easy food. They may have made the first pizzas. They put flatbreads on their metal shields. They added cheese. They added dates. They put their shields over a fire. This cooked the pizza.

Navy SEALs: Navy SEALs eat MREs. MRE means "meals ready to eat." They're packed foods. They're individual portions. They're made by the U.S. Department of Defense. They're given to soldiers. They replace canned foods. Navy SEALs work in extreme conditions. They carry heavy loads on foot. They serve on long missions. MREs are light. They don't need to be cooked. They can be eaten while moving. They can only eat MREs for 21 days. MREs are good for 3 years.

Move 4:

Immortals march to the beach. They march together. They have several sharp spears. They're holding them in their hands and belts. There are 10,000 Immortals. They're noisy.

Move 5:

Navy SEALs see the Immortals coming. They know they're outnumbered. They throw grenades. Some Immortals fall. But there are a lot of them. They keep coming.

Move 6:

Immortals throw their spears. They circle around the Navy SEALs. They take out their other spears. They stab downward.

Immortals and Navy SEALs are very loyal.

AND THE VICTOR IS . . .

What are their next moves?
Who do you think would win?

Immortals could win if:

- They watch their backs. Navy SEALs do sneak attacks. They're spies.
- They don't sleep at night. Navy SEALs like to attack at night.
- They get rid of Navy SEALs' gear. Navy SEALs have a lot of weapons. They have guns. They have a lot of high-tech tools.

Navy SEALs could win if:

- They get more Navy SEALs together. They need to combine the SEAL teams. There are many more Immortals than SEALs.
- They break Immortals apart. They need to focus more on mind games. They don't have as much manpower.
- They blow up the Immortals' covered wagons. This would cut off their supplies.

The SEALs make up less than 1 percent of the U.S. Navy. There are less than 3,000 SEALs.

Immortals: Top Champion

Cambyses II was the son of Cyrus the Great. He ruled the Persian Empire. He ruled over 7 years. He expanded the empire by taking over Egypt. He did this in the Battle of Pelusium. This battle took place in 525 BCE. Cambyses wanted to marry the pharaoh's daughter. Pharaohs are ancient Egyptian rulers. The pharaoh sent Cambyses another woman instead. Cambyses felt tricked. He was mad. He went to battle. He didn't just fight with force. He also liked to mess with people's minds. He knew Egyptians worshipped cats. He ordered the Immortals and other soldiers to paint cats on their shields. Egyptians saw the cats. They didn't want to fight. They didn't want to hurt the cats. Cambyses won the battle. No one knows how Cambyses died. One story said he lost his mind. He killed his brother. He cut his leg. His leg got infected. He died.

Navy SEALs: Top Champion

Chris Cassidy was born in 1970. He was born in Massachusetts. He graduated from the U.S. Naval Academy and Massachusetts Institute of Technology. He was a Navy SEAL for 10 years. He was a captain. He served several tours of duty. He fought in the war against terror. He fought in Afghanistan. He fought in the Mediterranean Sea. He fought in the Persian Gulf. But he wasn't happy with just saving Earth. He also went to space. He's a NASA astronaut. NASA is in charge of the U.S. space program. Cassidy was the chief of the Astronaut Office. He was the 500th person in space. He's the second Navy SEAL in space. He went on a couple of space missions. He did 6 spacewalks. Spacewalks are when astronauts work outside their ships. They float in space. Cassidy worked at the International Space Station. He spent 182 days in space. He's famous for taking a selfie from space. He did this in 2013.

Consider This!

THINK ABOUT IT!

- How are the Immortals and Navy SEALs alike? How are they different? Are they more alike or different? Why do you think so?
- If the Immortals and Navy SEALs lived at the same time, do you think they would've fought each other? If they did, who would've won? Why do you think so?
- Do you think you'd make a good soldier? Why or why not? If so, would you be a better Immortal or Navy SEAL? Why do you think so?
- Learn more about Navy SEALs training. Would you pass? Why or why not?
- Combine Immortals and Navy SEALs. Make a super soldier. What qualities would the super soldier have?

LEARN MORE!

- Dahm, Murray, and Peter Dennis (illust.). *Macedonian Phalangite Versus Persian Warrior: Alexander Confronts the Achaemenids, 334–331 BC*. Oxford: Osprey Publishing, 2019.
- McNab, Chris, and Adam Hook (illust.). *Greek Hoplite Versus Persian Warrior: 499–479 BC*. Oxford: Osprey Publishing, 2018.
- Newman, Patricia, *Navy SEALs: Elite Operations*. Minneapolis, MN: Lerner Publications, 2014.
- Slater, Lee. *Navy SEALs*. Minneapolis, MN: ABDO Publishing, 2016.

GLOSSARY

archery (AHR-chur-ee) activity involving the shooting of bows and arrows
camouflage (KAM-uh-flahzh) to hide or blend into the environment
elite (ih-LEET) a select group that is superior to others
grenades (gruh-NAYDZ) small hand bombs
guerilla warfare (guh-RIL-uh WOR-fair) irregular military actions, like hit-and-run tactics, carried out by small forces
immortal (ih-MOR-tuhl) being able to live forever
imperial (im-PEER-ee-uhl) of the empire
night vision goggles (NITE VIZH-uhn GAH-guhlz) special glasses that allow people to see at night
opponents (uh-POH-nuhnts) groups who compete against each other
parachute (PAH-ruh-shoot) to jump out of a plane with a tool that is like an umbrella's top used to slow down a fall
Persian (PUR-zhuhn) the ancient word for Iranian
rugged (RUHG-id) rocky and uneven
suspicious (suh-SPISH-uhs) wary, mistrustful; not sure
victor (VIK-tur) the winner
wicker (WIK-ur) flexible twigs that are braided or woven together to make things
warriors (WOR-ee-urz) fighters

INDEX

battlegrounds, 18–20
battles, 22–26

Cambyses, 30
Cassidy, Chris, 31

food, 25

Immortals, 30
    battlegrounds, 18–20
    battles, 22–26
    fun facts about, 11

how they win, 28
training, 8
weapons, 10, 21
what they wore, 10
who they were, 6–11

Navy SEALs, 31
    battlegrounds, 18–20
    battles, 22–26
    fun facts about, 17
    how they fight, 14
    how they win, 29

training, 13, 16, 24
weapons, 21
who they are, 12–17

opponents, 4

Persia, 7

victors, 4

weapons, 10, 21